A NOTE TO PARENTS

Early Step into Reading Books are designed for preschoolers and kindergartners who are just getting ready to read. The words are easy, the type is big, and the stories are packed with rhyme, rhythm, and repetition.

We suggest that you read this book to your child the first few times, pointing to each word as you go. Soon your child will start saying the words with you. And before long, he or she will try to read the story alone. Don't be surprised if your child uses the pictures to figure out the text—that's what they're there for! The important thing is to develop your child's confidence—and to show your child that reading is fun.

When your child is ready to move on, try the rest of the steps in our Step into Reading series. **Step 1 Books** (preschool–grade 1) feature the same easy-to-read type as the Early Step into Reading Books, but with more words per page. **Step 2 Books** (grades 1–3) are both longer and slightly more difficult, while **Step 3 Books** (grades 2–3) introduce readers to paragraphs and fully developed plot lines. **Step 4 Books** (grades 2–4) offer exciting nonfiction for the increasingly independent reader.

The grade levels assigned to the five steps are intended only as guides. Some children move through all five steps very rapidly; others climb the steps over a period of several years. Either way, these books will help your child "step into reading" in style!

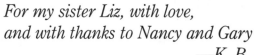
For Randi   —*G. H.*

For my sister Liz, with love,
and with thanks to Nancy and Gary
                   —*K. B.*

Library of Congress Cataloging-in-Publication Data
Herman, Gail. There is a town / by Gail Herman ; illustrated by Katy Bratun.
  p. cm. — (Early step into reading)
SUMMARY: Illustrations and simple text draw the reader into a family celebration at which a
girl receives a dollhouse.
ISBN 0-679-86439-3 (pbk.) — ISBN 0-679-96439-8 (lib. bdg.)
[1. Birthdays—Fiction. 2. Dollhouses—Fiction.] I. Bratun, Katy, ill. II. Title. III. Series.
PZ7.H4315Th 1996 [E]—dc20 94-34991

Early Step into Reading™

THERE IS A TOWN

by Gail Herman

illustrated by Katy Bratun

Random House 🏠 New York

There is a town.

And in this town,
there is a street.

And on this street,
there is a house.

And in this house,
there is a room.

And in this room,
there is a box.

And in this box, there is a house.

And in this house,
there is a room.

And in this room,
there is a box.

And in this box,
there is a cake.

And on this cake,
there are some words.

Words on the cake,

cake in the box,
box in the room,

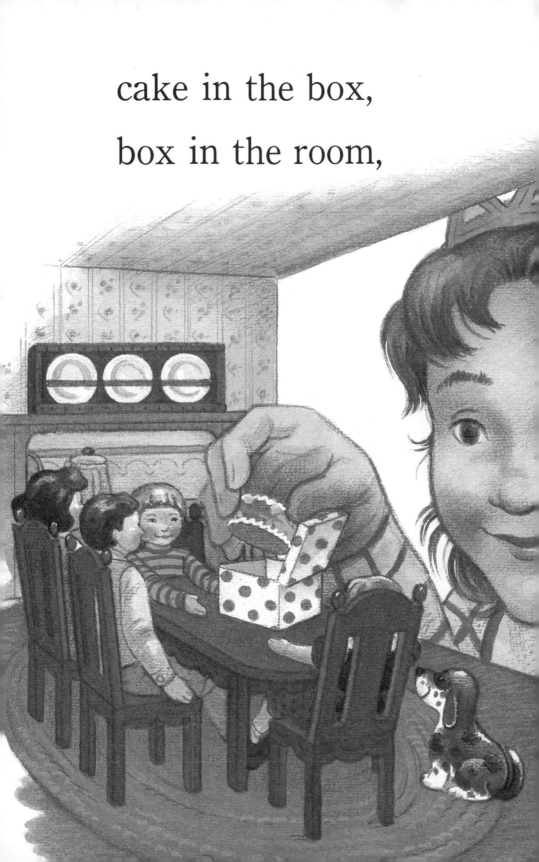

room in the house,

house in the box,

box in the room,

room in the house,

house on the street,

street in the town—

that goes to sleep.